Backyard Bandit Mystery

Beverly Lewis

D0111681

Beverly Lewis Books for Young Readers

PICTURE BOOKS

Annika's Secret Wish
Cows in the House
Just Like Mama

THE CUL-DE-SAC KIDS

The Double Dabble Surprise
The Chicken Pox Panic
The Crazy Christmas Angel Mystery
No Grown-ups Allowed
Frog Power
The Mystery of Case D. Luc
The Stinky Sneakers Mystery
Pickle Pizza
Mailbox Mania
The Mudhole Mystery
Fiddlesticks
The Crabby Cat Caper
Tarantula Toes
Green Gravy
Backyard Bandit Mystery
Tree House Trouble
The Creepy Sleep-Over
The Great TV Turn-Off
Piggy Party
The Granny Game
Mystery Mutt
Big Bad Beans
The Upside-Down Day
The Midnight Mystery

Katie and Jake and the Haircut Mistake

www.BeverlyLewis.com

THE CUL-DE-SAC KIDS

Backyard
Bandit Mystery

Beverly Lewis

BETHANY HOUSE PUBLISHERS
MINNEAPOLIS, MINNESOTA 55438

Backyard Bandit Mystery
Copyright © 1996
Beverly Lewis

Cover illustration by Paul Turnbaugh
Story illustrations by Janet Huntington

Published by Bethany House Publishers
11400 Hampshire Avenue South
Bloomington, Minnesota 55438

Bethany House Publishers is a division of
Baker Publishing Group, Grand Rapids, Michigan.

Printed in the United States of America

Library of Congress Cataloging-in-Publication Data

Lewis, Beverly, 1949–
    Backyard bandit mystery / by Beverly Lewis.
       p.   cm. — (The cul-de-sac kids)
    Summary: Even though Abby, the club president, is out of
town, Stacy and the rest of the Cul-de-sac Kids vote to have
a yard sale to raise money to buy flags for Flag Day.
    ISBN 1–55661–986–3 (pbk.)
    [1. Clubs—Fiction. 2. Garage sales—Fiction.
3. Mystery and detective stores.] I. Title. II. Series:
Lewis, Beverly, 1949–   Cul-de-sac kids.
PZ7.L58464Bag   1997
[Fic]—dc21
                                       97–21033
                                         CIP
                                            AC

For
Rochelle Glöege,
my editor and friend.
Happy Birthday!

I know a fine editor—Rochelle,
Her excellent work I must tell.
She edits; she writes,
Stays up late some nights.
What a wonderful person, Rochelle.

B. L.

THE CUL-DE-SAC KIDS

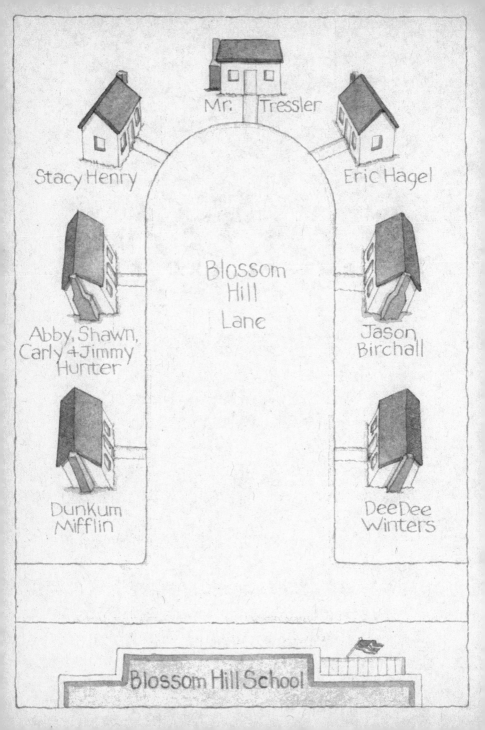

ONE

Stacy Henry couldn't sleep.

Whew! Too hot.

She was supposed to be sleeping in the teeny-weeny attic. With a teeny-tiny window that didn't open.

Stacy didn't mind, because her grandparents were visiting. They were staying in her bedroom.

But such heat! The attic bedroom was way too hot.

She fanned herself with a pillow.

She tried counting sheep. But thinking of sheep wool made her hotter.

Some fresh air would be nice. Some cool air.

Stacy sat up and lifted her hair off her neck.

Her puppy opened his eyes.

"I need a ponytail," she told him. "My head's too sweaty."

Sunday Funnies seemed to understand. He stood up and shook himself.

Stacy got out of bed and went to the hallway.

Fuzzy little Sunday Funnies followed.

They stood at the top of the steps and listened.

The house was quiet.

"Everyone's asleep," she whispered to the pup.

Then . . .

Tippity-pat-pat. She crept downstairs.

Jingle-pat-pat. Sunday Funnies came along.

Suddenly, Stacy stopped. So did her pup.

10

They heard a low rumble.

Grandpa's snoring. He said he got his best sleep that way.

"Let's be quiet," Stacy said to Sunday Funnies.

She tiptoed down the hall.

Flap-flop. Stacy's slippers slapped against her feet. They were big enough for an elephant. She tossed them off and went barefoot.

Inside her own room, Stacy sneaked past the round, snoring bodies. She hurried to the dresser.

Silently, she pulled open the top drawer. There, she found her hairbrush and a rubber band.

Then she went outside.

The top step was cooler than the wooden porch.

Stacy sat there and looked at the streetlight.

She wished for a breeze.

But the night was still. Breathless.

She brushed her hair back and made a ponytail.

AHH! Much better.

Sunday Funnies sat at her bare feet.

Stacy glanced down at him. "Some night we should sleep outside," she said. "It would be lots cooler."

She leaned back and stared at the sky.

"The Cul-de-sac Kids oughta have a sleep-out this summer," she said.

Sunday Funnies went and rolled in the cool grass.

"Smart boy," Stacy said.

She looked up and down Blossom Hill Lane.

The houses were dark. Middle-of-the-night dark.

No lights were shining from the windows. No sounds were springing from the doorways.

The whole cul-de-sac seemed gloomy.

Her best friend, Abby Hunter, was

camping this weekend. Abby's house next door looked lonely.

Stacy missed her friend.

She wondered if Abby was asleep yet. Or was *she* too hot? Or maybe homesick?

Stacy stared at the other houses.

Jason Birchall's was across the street.

Mr. Tressler's house was at the far end of the cul-de-sac.

Eric Hagel's house was between Mr. Tressler's and Jason's houses.

Dee Dee Winters' and Dunkum Mitchell's houses were at the other end of the cul-de-sac.

Besides being dark, the houses looked dull. Boring!

Stacy was thinking about Flag Day. Next Friday.

The houses on Blossom Hill Lane needed some American flags.

But Stacy was broke. She couldn't afford even *one* flag.

"Psst," she whispered to Sunday Funnies. "I know what we need. A yard sale! For all the Cul-de-sac Kids. Then we'll have enough money to buy flags!"

Her puppy jumped up and ran to her. He licked her face.

"Good idea, huh?" she said.

Then she glanced at Abby's house next door.

"Rats, it won't work," she said. "Abby's gone. The president of the Cul-de-sac Kids has to call the meeting. And we *all* have to vote."

Sunday Funnies squirmed in her arms.

"It was such a great idea," she said sadly. "Too bad."

TWO

It was early Saturday morning.

The sun peeked through the teeny-weeny attic window.

Yikes! Stacy felt warm licks on her face.

Sunday Funnies was wide awake.

"OK," she laughed. "I get the message."

As soon as Stacy yawned, she remembered her idea.

"I'm gonna talk to Dunkum today," she said.

Dunkum's real name was Edward

Mitchell. He was the tallest and best hoop shooter around. Everyone called him Dunkum.

"Maybe we could have a club meeting after all," she told her puppy.

But Stacy felt funny inside. Abby and her brothers and sister were part of the club, too. It wouldn't be fair to vote without them.

Would it?

Sunday Funnies turned his head and looked up at her. He seemed to think her idea was OK.

Stacy wasn't too sure. She'd have to check with Dunkum. *He* would know what to do.

★ ★ ★

Stacy couldn't wait to finish breakfast.

She poured a glass of juice. Then she sliced a banana on her cereal.

At last, she hurried down to Dunkum's house.

17

He was outside shooting baskets. "Hi, Stacy. What's up?" he asked.

"I have a great idea," she said.

He stopped shooting. "What is it?"

"We need to have a club meeting," she told him.

"Right now?" He glanced up the street. "Looks like the rest of the Cul-de-sac Kids are sleeping in."

"Summers and Saturdays," she said under her breath.

"What's the meeting about?" he asked.

Stacy told him the Flag Day idea. "We need to jazz up Blossom Hill Lane," she said. "With flags."

Dunkum grinned. "Cool idea!"

"Only one problem. We have no money," she said.

"There's a little in the club fund," Dunkum said. He put his ball down and ran into the house.

Stacy hoped there was enough money to buy seven flags.

She looked at the houses again.
Flags would really spiff things up.
She crossed her fingers.

★ ★ ★

Stacy waited.
And waited.
And waited some more.
What's taking so long? she wondered.
At last, Dunkum came outside.
His face looked like a prune.
"What's wrong?" Stacy asked.
"I counted the money twice." Dunkum shrugged his shoulders. "I thought there was more."
"How much *is* there?" asked Stacy.
"Only two dollars and fifty-three cents. Mostly dimes and nickels," replied Dunkum.
Stacy uncrossed her fingers. "Not enough for seven flags."
"Not even close." Dunkum picked up his basketball.

"What about a fund-raiser?" said Stacy. "A yard sale . . . at my house? This afternoon?"

Dunkum was silent. He aimed high, shot, and made it.

He looked at her. "Abby's gone," he said. "We can't vote without our president."

"I thought of that, too," said Stacy. "Besides, Carly, Shawn, and Jimmy aren't here to vote, either."

"You're right," Dunkum said.

She watched him make some fancy moves.

"Well, what if we broke the rules? Just once?" she suggested.

Dunkum didn't say anything. He kept shooting.

Stacy kept talking. "What do you really think?"

"Abby probably wouldn't mind," he said.

"Should we talk to the others about it?" she asked.

Dunkum nodded. "Wanna?"

"Why not?" Stacy said with a grin.

But she had a strange feeling.

They'd never done *this* before!

THREE

Stacy stared at the beanbag president's chair. Abby Hunter's seat.

Poof! Stacy sat down too hard.

"The meeting will come to order," she said.

Dee Dee raised her hand. "Is this a real meeting?" She looked around the room. "Because if it is, there's four of us missing."

Stacy nodded. "You're right."

Dunkum tried to explain to little Dee Dee. "We wanna buy some flags for Flag Day." He glanced over at Stacy. "It's a great idea. We just wanna talk about it."

Eric Hagel and Jason Birchall liked the idea. They both said so.

"Why do we have to vote?" Jason asked.

"Yeah," said Eric. "Abby doesn't care if we make some money. It would be a good surprise!"

"When the cat's away, the mice'll *pay*," Jason said.

Dee Dee giggled.

Stacy didn't laugh. "So, is it settled?" she asked everyone.

Five heads nodded *yes*.

"Well, are we gonna vote?" Dunkum asked.

"Go for it!" shouted Jason.

"OK," said Stacy. "How many in favor of a yard sale?"

Five hands went up.

"How many want the yard sale to start today?" she asked.

Same five hands.

"Yes!" said Dunkum. "We're in business."

"Yay!" Stacy said. "Let's start gathering up our old loot. Anything we don't want."

"Hey! Your trash could be *my* treasure," Jason teased.

Dunkum and Eric agreed.

So did the girls.

"This'll be so-o cool," Dee Dee said.

"I'm gonna search for hidden treasure," Eric said. And he went right home.

So did everyone else.

★ ★ ★

Stacy hurried into the house. "Do we have anything to sell?" she asked her mom.

"Like what?" her mom said, smiling.

"You know, trash or treasures. For a yard sale," Stacy said.

Her mother thought for a moment. "I

don't think so," she said.

"Ple-e-ease, will you look?" Stacy pleaded.

"What's the sale for?" asked her mother.

"Money for Flag Day," answered Stacy. "The Cul-de-sac Kids wanna buy flags for every house on the block."

"Flags?" said Grandpa. "What a nice idea."

Stacy smiled. "I thought so, too."

"Where will you put the flags?" asked her granny.

"On all the porches," Stacy explained.

Grandpa got off the couch and headed down the hall.

"Where are you going, dear?" asked Granny.

"To scout around," Grandpa said.

"Where?" Granny asked.

"In the suitcase," Grandpa answered.

Granny's eyebrows flew up. "Oh no!"

"It's OK," Stacy said. "I'm sure he'll find something."

"That's what I'm afraid of," replied Granny.

"I'll go help him," Stacy offered.

Now her mother was frowning. "Better let Grandpa do his own looking," she said.

Stacy glanced at Granny. She was *really* frowning now.

"Oh, sorry," Stacy said quietly.

She knew she better stay out of it.

So she went to the attic.

It was time for some scouting of her own.

FOUR

Later, Stacy and Grandpa hid out in the attic.

Some of their old treasures were piled on the bed.

"Don't let Granny catch you with these," Grandpa whispered.

Stacy looked through her grandpa's things.

There was a bottle of men's cologne, nearly full.

Stacy twisted the cap and gave a sniff. "Don't you want this?" she asked.

"Never liked the smell," he said with a

grin. "Granny's the one who bought it."

Stacy shrugged. "Won't she be upset?"

"Ah, she'll get over it." He waved his hand.

"What if she doesn't?" Stacy asked.

"She'll just have to buy it back." He was laughing.

Next he held up his pajama top.

"I think you might need that, Grandpa," said Stacy.

He laughed. "In this heat? No chance!"

It *was* hot for June. Especially June in Colorado.

"Just skip the pajama top and sleep in your undershirt," Stacy suggested.

"Hallelujah!" said Grandpa.

And he went downstairs.

I don't wanna get in trouble, thought Stacy.

But she wasn't too worried. She remembered what Grandpa said. If Granny missed his stuff, she could just buy it back.

Hallelujah!

★ ★ ★

Before lunch, Dee Dee came over.

Stacy showed off some of her treasures. She showed some of her not-so-great treasures, too.

There was an old fish bowl.

Used magazines.

Some baby books with thick pages.

A beanbag angel with wings.

Three sets of skirts and blouses. Two sweaters.

Dee Dee held up one of the skirts. "I like this one," she said.

"It's not for sale . . . not yet," Stacy said.

Dee Dee folded the skirt and put it away. "What about this?" She held up the beanbag angel. "It's real cute."

Stacy nodded. "Abby gave me that a long time ago."

"Don't you want it anymore?" asked

30

Dee Dee. "It's so-o sweet."

"I'm tired of it," Stacy said.

Dee Dee played with the angel. She made it fly around. "What'll Abby say?" she asked.

Stacy laughed. "Abby won't care about a silly little beanie angel."

"Are ya sure?" Dee Dee asked.

"Of course," Stacy replied. "Besides, it's really old."

Dee Dee put the angel back in the pile. "OK, then."

"Let's see *your* things," said Stacy.

Dee Dee's face lit up. She pulled out an old cat collar.

"This was Mister Whiskers' baby collar," she said. "Think it'll sell?"

"Sure will," Stacy replied.

There was more. Several old guitar albums.

Three stuffed animals—a parrot, fish, and a bee.

And a pink piggy bank.

"You've got some good stuff," Stacy told Dee Dee.

Dee Dee smiled. "Wait'll ya see Dunkum's loot."

"Really?" Stacy said.

"Come with me," said Dee Dee.

And the two of them hurried down the cul-de-sac.

★ ★ ★

Dunkum had a bunch, all right.

There were two baseball gloves.

Toy cars and trucks—a toy box full.

A stack of comic books.

And an old radio with star antennas.

"Nice things," Stacy said.

"Not to me," Dunkum said. "I've got new toys."

Dee Dee picked up the old radio. "Does this work?"

Dunkum plugged it in. Music blared out.

Dee Dee clicked her fingers. "Hey, cool," she said.

Then Stacy, Dee Dee, and Dunkum headed to Eric's house.

"I wonder if Eric's grandpa gave him anything for the sale," Stacy said.

"How come?" Dunkum asked as they walked.

"Well, I was thinking about Grandpa's pajama top," she said. "It would be nice if someone donated a bottom."

"A *what*?" Dee Dee giggled.

Dunkum laughed, too.

Stacy tried to explain. But they were laughing too much.

At last, they stopped.

Stacy told about her grandpa and his pajamas. "He gets too warm in the summertime," she said.

"He oughta sleep in his *birthday suit*!" Dee Dee said.

Stacy and Dunkum howled. They laughed so hard, they could barely walk.

They passed Jason Birchall's house. Next door was Eric's house.

Jason and his frog were there, too. "What's so funny?" he asked. "I heard you laughing all the way up the cul-de-sac."

Dee Dee told about the pajama problem. "We need a complete set of pj's. For the yard sale."

Jason looked confused. "What's so funny about that?"

Dunkum tried not to laugh. "Maybe we'll borrow *your* pj's, Jason."

Jason rolled his eyes and backed away. "Whoa, don't look at me!" he said. "I like to cook breakfast in my pajamas."

"Why don't you use a frying pan? Isn't that kinda messy?" Eric said.

Now they were all laughing.

Even Jason.

Stacy glanced up the street. "Hey, look," she said.

The kids turned to see where she was pointing.

"Mr. Tressler's got pajamas," she said. "I can see them from here."

The striped pj's were hanging on the clothesline.

"I wonder if Mr. Tressler wants to donate something," Dunkum said.

"Let's go find out," Jason said.

Stacy and Dunkum looked at each other.

"Why don't *you* ask him?" they said to Jason.

Jason shook his head. "This wasn't my idea."

"OK, I'll go," Dee Dee said.

She started down the sidewalk. Then she turned back.

"What am I supposed to say?" she asked.

Stacy sighed. "C'mon. I'll go with you." And she did.

FIVE

It was right after lunch. Time for the yard sale.

The sun was hot.

Stacy made lemonade for everyone.

Dunkum brought a folding table.

Eric borrowed his mother's old table-cloth.

Jason brought a long electric cord. It was to plug in Dunkum's radio.

"Music always livens things up," Jason said.

Everyone agreed.

Dee Dee sat in the grass and made a

sale sign. She drew the letters carefully.

Dunkum watched. "The *e*'s are inside out," he told her.

Stacy went over to look. "Who cares?" she said. "We're just kids, right?"

Dee Dee smiled up at Stacy. "You're nice," Dee Dee said.

Stacy picked up the sign. "You did an excellent job."

Dee Dee got up and stuck the sign on the tablecloth.

"We need some nickels, dimes, and pennies," Dunkum said.

"What for?" Jason asked.

"To make money, we have to start with some," Dunkum explained. "We might need to make change."

"What about the two dollars and fifty-three cents in our club fund?" asked Stacy.

"Good thinking," Dunkum said. He dashed out the backyard gate.

Together, Dee Dee and Stacy arranged the sale table.

They displayed Mr. Tressler's striped pj top. Stacy put it beside her grandpa's green pajama top.

"Now we've got two tops and no bottoms," Dee Dee said.

Stacy and Dee Dee giggled about it. They had fun sorting everything.

Stacy stepped back for a look. "This is really a good idea," she said.

Dee Dee grinned. "If you must say so yourself!"

"Well, it's *my* idea," said Stacy.

"That's just what I mean," Dee Dee said.

Jason came over and turned up the radio. He danced around. Then he said, "Let someone else toot your horn, Stacy."

"Oh, I get it," Stacy muttered. She felt silly about bragging.

Real silly.

★ ★ ★

The Cul-de-sac Kids posted signs all

over Blossom Hill Lane.

They told their parents. And their friends.

Now they were ready for customers. Lots of them.

Stacy could almost see the flags flying. Seven beautiful flags for Flag Day.

The Cul-de-sac Kids waited.

And waited.

The sun got hotter.

And hotter.

They poured glasses of lemonade. One after another.

"We oughta charge ourselves for the drinks," Dee Dee said.

Dunkum nodded. "Why didn't I think of that?"

Stacy agreed. "It would be *one* way to make money."

"Yeah, because nobody's showin' up," Dee Dee said.

Eric wiped his forehead. "It's too hot, that's why."

"We need some shade," Dunkum said.

Stacy remembered something in the attic. "I might have just what we need." She darted into the house.

Upstairs, she crawled on her knees. She looked under the little attic bed.

There it was.

She stretched her arm as far as she could.

The old striped canvas wasn't very big, but it might work.

Now she needed some tools.

She called for Grandpa. "I need a little help."

Grandpa came to the attic in his undershirt and some red shorts. He was very round in certain places.

Stacy tried not to stare.

It was too hot for Grandpa to care.

"Here we are." He found just what they needed: a hammer and nails.

Grandpa headed for the kitchen door.

41

Stacy stopped. "Uh, are you going out-side?" she asked.

Grandpa curled the canopy under one arm. "Show me where you want this thing," he said.

Stacy took a deep breath. Grandpa was going out dressed like *that*!

She held the door open for him. And she carried the hammer and nails outside.

Grandpa called, "Hey, kids!"

Everyone turned to look.

"Gonna have yourselves some shade," he told them.

The Cul-de-sac Kids cheered.

"Hoo-ray for Stacy's grandpa," Jason said.

Stacy put on a smile. She tried not to think about Grandpa's undershirt. And not his red jogging shorts.

Dee Dee whispered, "Isn't that his underwear?"

Stacy heard it and glanced at her plump grandpa. "Those are jogging shorts," she told Dee Dee. "Red summer shorts."

"Oh," said Dee Dee. "Looks like—"

"Nevermind," Stacy said. "Let's help."

The girls found a ladder in the garage.

Dunkum and Eric carried it to the sale table.

Grandpa stepped on the bottom rung. He shook it around. The shaking made his stomach jiggle. Some of the other chunky places did, too.

Eric steadied the ladder.

Grandpa laughed. "How old's this thing, anyway?"

"Be careful," Stacy warned him. Then she handed the hammer up.

The boys helped Grandpa with the canvas. They stretched it over some boards and hammered away.

Jason and Dee Dee handed up the nails. One by one.

Stacy held her breath till the job was done.

"Awesome idea!" Jason said, looking at it.

"It's like an awning," Stacy said. "Thanks, Grandpa."

"Any old time," he said.

Then he went inside the house.

The kids hollered their "thank-you's."

Now they could have their super sale.

Shady and fine.

Grandpa's real cool, thought Stacy.

SIX

It was the middle of the afternoon.

"We're running out of lemonade," Jason said.

"I'll make some more," said Stacy. She hurried to the house.

Grandpa was sitting near the kitchen fan. "Any customers yet?" he asked.

"It's too hot, but they'll come," Stacy said.

Granny came in the room. "Who's coming to what?" she asked.

Stacy explained about the yard sale. "Go out and have a look," she said.

"Don't mind if I do," Granny said.

But Grandpa was waving his hands at Stacy. He was trying to signal her.

Stacy finally caught on. "Oh . . . uh," she started to say.

Too late. Granny was already heading for her purse.

"Sorry about that," Stacy told Grandpa. "I forgot."

He shook his head. "Who knows, maybe she won't spot my old things."

Stacy laughed. "Granny's real sharp. She'll notice, all right."

Soon, Granny came back with her cane and her purse. "I'm gonna have me some fun," she said.

Out she went.

Grandpa went to the window. He stood there fussing.

Stacy stirred sugar into the lemonade. "Wanna taste?" she asked.

Grandpa came over. "Sure do," he said and sipped a little.

Then he frowned and thought about it. "Well, I don't know. Give me a little more."

Stacy poured more lemonade.

Grandpa drank all of it.

Then he thought and frowned. "I think it's still too sour."

Stacy added a pinch more sugar. "Now try it."

Grandpa held out his glass. "Give me plenty," he said.

Then Stacy began to giggle. "You don't fool me, Grandpa. Why didn't you ask for a full glass to start with?"

Grandpa chuckled and winked at her.

"My friends are dying of thirst," Stacy said. "I'd better get back outside." She carried the tall pitcher carefully.

Granny passed her on the garden path.

But Stacy was too busy to look. She didn't notice if Granny had made any purchases.

Stacy set the pitcher down on the sale table.

The kids came running.

She poured one glass after another. Then she sat under the table and fanned herself. "Maybe it's just too hot for a yard sale."

"No way!" Dee Dee said. "It's a totally cool idea!"

"Yep," said Jason. "And we just made some bucks."

Stacy couldn't believe it. "We did?"

Dunkum filled her in. "Your granny bought several things. She's a big spender."

Stacy laughed. "Let me guess," she said. "A half pair of pj's?"

"You got it," Eric chimed in. "And some smelly perfume, too."

"Anything else?" asked Stacy.

Eric was smiling. "I bought your bean-bag angel. For fifty cents!" He pushed the angel into his pocket. Its halo stuck out.

"Do ya think Abby will like it?"

Stacy gulped. "Did you say 'Abby'?" she squeaked.

"Yeah. It's gonna be her birthday present from me," Eric said.

"You're giving my angel to *Abby*?" said Stacy.

Eric nodded his head. "Tomorrow, when she gets back from camping," he said.

Dee Dee wrinkled her nose and stared at Stacy.

Stacy looked at Dee Dee and made another gulp.

They'd sold the present Abby had given to *her*. And Eric was using it for a birthday gift.

I have to get it back, she thought. But how?

SEVEN

It was supper time. The kids went home to eat. They left the yard sale table all alone.

"See ya," Jason shouted.

"'Bye," said Stacy.

"Have a good supper," Eric called.

The angel stuck out of his pocket.

What'll I do? Stacy worried.

Then her mother called, "Ready to eat?"

"I'm coming," Stacy said. She clunked into the house.

She smelled fried chicken. But she didn't feel hungry.

Sniff. Something else smelled good.

Granny grinned. "Such a nice back-yard sale," she said.

"Glad you liked it," Stacy told her.

Grandpa winked. He smelled just like the yard sale cologne.

Stacy wondered about the pajama top. But she didn't say a word. Not a single one.

Poor Grandpa. Now he'd have to wear his pj top for sure.

Stacy thought and thought. Wearing pajama tops or bottoms wasn't a problem. But something else was.

Eric was going to give Abby the bean-bag angel. *That* was a problem. A BIG one.

I have to stop him, Stacy decided.

Determined, she gave him a call.

"I need my angel back," she said.

"Why?" Eric asked.

"I shouldn't have sold it," she said. "That's why."

"Well, you did. And now I have to eat supper," he said.

Eric hung up.

Stacy wanted to run across the street. Right to his house—right this minute!

★ ★ ★

After supper, Stacy took an old sheet outside. She wanted to cover up the sale stuff. She wanted to make sure everything was safe.

But something seemed strange.

She looked all around the table. "This is weird," she whispered to herself.

The table seemed empty. *Very* empty.

She thought of all the cool sale items. Dunkum's and Eric's things. Dee Dee's stuff.

"Where *is* everything?" she said out loud.

Then she glanced around, feeling

worried. Had a thief come during supper?

Carefully, she inspected the table.

Two of Dunkum's baseball gloves were missing. So was his radio.

Dee Dee's cat collar was gone. The bee stuffed animal and guitar records were missing. And a bunch of other things.

"I don't remember selling any of those," she said.

Stacy searched everywhere.

Where could they be? she wondered.

Then an idea struck.

Maybe the kids had taken some of the things home. For safekeeping. Maybe *that's* what had happened.

Stacy thought hard.

Nope, the kids wouldn't do that. Not without telling her.

So Granny was the one to talk to. Maybe *she* had bought all those things.

Maybe . . .

Stacy checked around for the money box. Gone.

Dunkum probably had it. He was in charge of the club fund.

She hurried back inside.

"We're ready for dessert," said her mother.

"Where's Granny?" Stacy asked.

"Down the hall," her mother said.

Stacy found Granny in the bedroom. She asked about the missing sale items.

"I bought two things," Granny said. She held up two fingers. "Nothing else."

Stacy didn't need to be told what they were.

"Are we ready for dessert?" her mother called.

Stacy hurried back to the kitchen. She picked up the wall phone. "First, I have to call Dunkum," she said. "It's very important."

Grandpa chuckled. "What's more important than strawberry shortcake?" he teased.

"A backyard bandit," Stacy said. "I

think someone's stealing our sale stuff."

Grandpa scratched his head. "What a horrible thing. Can't kids have any fun these days?"

"I'm gonna find out what happened," Stacy told him.

He got up and peered out the back door. "Who'd want to do such a thing?"

"That's what *I* wanna know," Stacy said.

She punched the phone numbers.

Dunkum answered. "Hello?"

"Hi, it's Stacy. I think someone's ripping us off!" She explained about the missing things.

"Maybe you should do some spying," he suggested. "Maybe the thief will come back."

"Good idea!" she said. "I'll spy tonight . . . after dark."

"Be careful," Dunkum warned.

"I will," she said. "I promise."

Stacy hung up and ate her dessert.

Then she headed outside.

But she could only think of one thing. The yellow beanbag angel. A gift from her very best friend.

EIGHT

The moon was full. Too bright for spying.

Stacy crept outside anyway.

She found an empty trash can. But it was too far from the sale table. So she dragged it across the backyard.

She thought, *good idea*. And crawled inside the smelly garbage can.

For a few minutes, she pinched her nose shut. But breathing through her mouth was horrible.

Who knows what might fly in! she thought.

Wicked worms and bugs and things. All of them might be crawling inside the trash can.

Icksville! Stacy shivered.

She let her nose do the breathing.

But . . .

Pee-uu-wee! What a sick smell.

Quickly, she lifted the lid for some fresh air.

She saw two shadows. Kid-sized ones.

Who were they?

Stacy inched the lid off the trash can. She leaned forward and listened.

The shadows were whispering.

Were they inspecting the sale stuff? Plotting to steal?

She perked up her ears. The voices were familiar.

Dee Dee and Eric! And they were discussing something.

Stacy listened hard. She leaned and watched.

"I'll trade my parrot for your leather

coin case," a voice said.

It was a tiny voice. A Dee Dee Winters voice!

Had Stacy heard right? Did Dee Dee want to *trade* something?

Stacy kept listening. She couldn't believe her ears.

Now the boy shadow was talking. Sounded like Eric Hagel.

Stacy couldn't hear everything he was saying. But it was about Dee Dee's stuffed animal. Her parrot—all blue, green, and orange.

What's going on? Stacy wondered.

She watched closely.

Now Dee Dee was holding her cat up to the table. "Did ya ever see such a cool backyard sale?" she said.

Mew, replied Mister Whiskers.

Dee Dee giggled. "You know a good sale when ya see it," she said.

Eric laughed. He held up his hamster. "Fran the Ham says there oughta be free lettuce to munch." He made his voice sound twittery. Like a hamster.

Dee Dee and Eric went on and on. They were talking back and forth, pretending.

At last, Eric spoke in his regular voice. "Won't our flags look great for Flag Day?" he said.

"Stacy's idea was real cool," Dee Dee answered.

Stacy felt a kink in her leg. She tried to stretch inside the trash can.

I have to get out of here, she decided.

But . . .

She leaned too hard.

Bang-a clank!

The trash can fell over, and Stacy tumbled out.

Eric and Dee Dee screamed and ran away.

Stacy crawled out of the trash can. "So much for spying," she muttered.

She stood there alone in the moon-light.

Rats!

She brushed herself off. No more icky insects crawling on her!

Silently, she ran to the house.

She felt terribly upset. And she smelled like a trash heap.

So she took a bath and went to bed.

Later, in the darkness, she reached for her beanbag angel.

Then she remembered. . . .

It was gone.

Sold to Eric for fifty cents!

NINE

It was Sunday morning. Church day.

But Stacy's thoughts were somewhere else.

"I have to talk to Eric before Sunday school," she told her puppy. Sunday Funnies had already found the Sunday paper. And the comics.

She hurried to the teeny-weeny attic window. She pushed her face against it. "Can't see a thing," she muttered.

So she combed her hair and got dressed.

Before anyone else was up, she went outside. She dashed across the street.

Brr-i-i-i-n-g!

She rang the doorbell one long ring.

Eric just *had* to answer it.

She waited.

And waited.

At last, he opened the door. "What are you doing over here?" he asked.

Stacy stared at him. Blond hairs were sticking out. Every which way!

"I came for my beanbag angel," she said.

He raised his eyebrows. "It's mine. I already told you."

"Well, sorry," Stacy said.

Eric frowned. "I paid for it, Stacy."

"I know, but I want it back," she said.

He argued. "It was on the sale table!"

Stacy shook her head. "Well, I never should've put it there."

"But you did." Eric bunched up his mouth.

"I HAVE TO HAVE IT BACK!" shouted Stacy.

She crossed her arms and made a big frown. She tapped her toe and waited.

Surely, Eric would come to his senses.

"Well? Are you gonna give it back?" she asked.

"I said it's mine," Eric grouched.

"You'll be sorry, Eric Hagel," she said. And marched home.

★ ★ ★

After church, Stacy saw Eric again. He was standing outside, waiting for his mother.

"Did you listen to the preacher today?" she asked.

"Uh-huh," he answered.

"Well? Are you gonna be a cheerful giver?" she asked.

Eric stared at her. "Are *you* gonna be a grumpy giver?"

Stacy didn't answer. Eric was right about her, but it didn't sound so nice.

Then she remembered the missing

sale stuff. "Have you heard about the robbery? I think there's a bandit in our cul-de-sac," she said.

Eric scratched his head. "What are you talking about?"

She told him. "Lots of our sale stuff has disappeared."

"Since when?" he asked.

"Last night, during supper. That's when the robber must've come," she explained.

He shook his head. "Don't know anything," he said.

"Some of *your* stuff is gone, too," she said.

Eric's eyes got big. "My stuff? Don't you mean the stuff I *donated*? I'm no grumpy giver," he insisted.

"Very funny, Eric," she said.

And she spun away on her heels.

TEN

Stacy looked at her watch.

Almost two o'clock.

Eric was being a big pain. He refused to give back the angel. He just wouldn't.

Stacy felt horrible.

Abby Hunter would be home soon. Very soon.

Stacy didn't know what to do. She couldn't get Eric to budge.

Besides that, there was a mystery to solve.

Who *was* the backyard bandit?

Stacy didn't know.

She raced down the cul-de-sac to Dee Dee's house. "We have a problem," she said.

Dee Dee opened the door and let her in. "What's wrong?"

"There's a bandit on the loose," Stacy said.

"A what?" Dee Dee's eyes were wide.

"Lots of our sale stuff is missing," she explained.

"Oh, that." Dee Dee grinned.

Stacy stared at her. "Do *you* know who the bandit is?" she asked.

"Follow me," Dee Dee said.

They went upstairs.

"Is this what you're missing?" Dee Dee asked.

There was Dunkum's old radio on the dresser.

"What's it doing here?" asked Stacy.

Dee Dee explained. "I traded some of my stuff with the boys."

Stacy couldn't believe her ears.

"How can we make any money *that* way?" she demanded.

"Oh, there's plenty of money," Dee Dee said.

"There is?" Stacy said, surprised.

"Sure! Your granny paid bunches of money. She bought that smelly old cologne. Your grandpa's pajama top, too," said Dee Dee.

"For how much?" Stacy asked.

"Twenty bucks," answered Dee Dee.

"Twenty? That's way too much," said Stacy.

"I know, but she wouldn't listen," Dee Dee said.

Stacy couldn't believe her ears.

"Your granny wanted to make some nice kids happy," Dee Dee explained. "That's just what she said."

"Nobody told *me* about this," Stacy said.

Dee Dee shook her head. "I guess you were busy makin' lemonade."

Stacy thought about everything. "So, we'll buy the flags with Granny's money?"

Dee Dee grinned. "Yep."

"Wow," Stacy said.

"Real cool," Dee Dee added.

"Well, there's only one other problem now," Stacy said.

Dee Dee looked up at her. "The bean-bag angel?" she asked.

Stacy nodded. "I need to get it back. What can I do?"

"I have an idea," Dee Dee said. And she whispered in Stacy's ear.

Stacy listened carefully.

Then she said, "You're right. Thanks for a great idea!"

And up the street she ran—to see Eric about the angel.

★ ★ ★

When Stacy found Eric, he was playing with his hamster. A teeny-tiny cat collar was on Fran the Ham's neck.

"Nice trade," Stacy said. She meant the cat collar.

Eric looked up. "Oh, you heard?"

She nodded. "You traded your treasures. Wanna trade something with me?" she asked.

"Whatcha got?" he said.

"A whole sale table full," she replied.

Eric smiled a strange little smile. "Really? You'd give me *everything* on the table?"

Stacy nodded. "Only if you give back my beanie angel."

Eric rubbed his head. "You must really want it," he said.

"Sure do," she said.

"What's so special about it?" he asked.

She took a deep breath. "Abby gave it to me a long time ago."

Eric's eyes nearly popped out. "*Abby* gave it to you?"

"That's why," she said softly.

"Why didn't you tell me?" Eric said.

"I should've," Stacy replied. "I'm sorry."

Eric grinned at her. "This is our secret, OK?"

"Thanks," Stacy said.

"And you can forget about trading the sale stuff," he said. "I don't want it."

Stacy smiled. "You're a cheerful giver."

"Here, hold my hamster." Eric ran inside to get the angel.

Stacy held Fran the Ham carefully.

At that moment, Abby and her family rode up the cul-de-sac. The Hunter family waved to her.

Stacy called to them, "Welcome home!"

Abby leaned out the van window. "Did I miss anything?" she asked.

"You just wait," Stacy said, grinning.

Abby smiled back. "Double dabble good," she said. Then she picked up two suitcases and ran to her house.

Fran the Ham made twittering sounds in Stacy's hand. Nothing special. Just cute little hamster noises.

Stacy leaned over and whispered in the teeny-weeny ear. "Flag Day's gonna be super. Thanks to a super-duper Granny."

She thought for a second. "Thanks to Eric, too."

Stacy felt great. Even if she had to say so herself.

THE CUL-DE-SAC KIDS SERIES
Don't miss #16!
TREE HOUSE TROUBLE

Abby Hunter and Stacy Henry are busy with a spring project. They're building a tree house (with a little help from Stacy's grandpa).

When the hideaway is finished, the girls discover that a very cool tree house can cause very BIG trouble. Especially when they start posting signs that read: "Definitely No Boys Allowed!"

What will happen to their faithful motto: "The Cul-de-sac Kids stick together"? Is this the end for Abby's club on Blossom Hill Lane?

ABOUT THE AUTHOR

Beverly Lewis thinks yard sales are super. "Where can you have so much fun for a dime?" she says.

Some "treasures" she's found are a computer desk, a toy train with tracks, bikes, and a beanbag angel.

Beverly thanks her sister for a great idea. (Barbara thought the Cul-de-sac Kids should trade their treasures in this book.)

If you like mystery and humor, read *all* the Cul-de-sac Kids books. You'll be glad you did!

Girls Like You—
PURSUING OLYMPIC DREAMS!

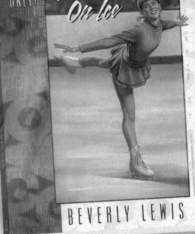

Don't miss the new series of books from Beverly Lewis called GIRLS ONLY (GO!). In this fun-loving series, you'll meet Olympic hopefuls like Livvy, Jenna, and Heather, girls training to compete in popular Olympic sports like figure-skating, gymnastics, and ice-dancing. Along the way, they tackle the same kinds of problems and tough choices you do—with friends and family, at school and at home. You'll love cheering on these likable girls as they face life's challenges and triumphs!

GIRLS ONLY (GO!)

Dreams on Ice	Follow the Dream
Only the Best	Better Than Best
A Perfect Match	Photo Perfect
Reach for the Stars	Star Status

POPULAR WITH SPORTS-MINDED GIRLS EVERYWHERE!

www.BeverlyLewis.com

*with David Lewis